I0572616

The Green Heart

Our Path to Peace

written by Laura Stoner Delavie

illustrated by Juliet Frost

ANAHATA PUBLISHING ♥ ALCEMIS, LLC ♥ MINNEAPOLIS

Published on the traditional homeland of the Dakota people in Minnesota, United States of America, by Anahata Publishing, an imprint of ALCEMIS, LLC. Send permission requests to: Permissions—Anahata Publishing, ALCEMIS, LLC, 3800 American Blvd W, Suite 1500 PMB 3312, Bloomington, MN 55431.

This is a work of fiction. Names, characters, places, events, and incidents are either the product of the author's imagination or used in a fictitious manner. The information in this book is distributed on an "as is" basis, without warranty. Neither the author nor the publisher shall have any liability to any person or entity with respect to any loss or damage caused or alleged to be caused, directly or indirectly, by the information contained in this book or related supplemental materials/resources.

The content is not intended to be a substitute for professional medical, mental health, or relationship advice, diagnosis, or treatment. Never disregard professional medical or therapeutic advice or delay in seeking it because of something you have read in this book or related supplemental materials/resources.

References:
The Cherokee legend of two wolves, passed down through oral tradition, is a lesson about how our choices shape who we become. The author originally heard the legend during a retreat.
Frankl, Viktor E. *Man's Search for Meaning*. Beacon Press, 1985 (ISBN 0-671-66736-X).
Hillesum, Etty. *De nagelaten geschriften van Etty Hillesum 1941-1943*. Uitgeverij Balans, 1986. English translation by Google Translate.

First Edition
ISBN: 979-8-9933313-0-0 (hardcover) / ISBN: 979-8-9933313-1-7 (paperback) / ISBN: 979-8-9933313-2-4 (eBook)
Library of Congress Control Number: 2025921267

Please visit: www.ALCEMIS.com/thegreenheart

For Chad, my love, my puzzle piece,
whose heart is full of joy and love.
Big Green Heart

The Wartons began invading civilized lands across
the Middle East and Europe more than 6,000 years
ago and caused great destruction.

Century after century, their violent, dominating,
and oppressive behaviors became normal
for everyone across the planet...
except for the Quartics.

Honoring her Quartic ancestors,
Martine went further than all others
to save Earth and humanity from the Wartons.

She was determined to create a world where
peace and prosperity would be experienced by all.

Sometimes, though, Martine wondered sadly,
"How will fighting the Wartons manifest peace?"
It made no sense. For thousands of years,
fighting and war had only led to more hate,
oppression, violence, depression, and destruction.

At the Parthenon, a place built
to celebrate victory in war, Martine met Carter,
another Quartic known for winning against the Wartons.
Seeking better ways to create peace, he joined Martine and
they traveled into the countryside to plan their next steps.

Crossing over the River Zarthan,
they found the Artemis Spring.
Needing a break from their long journey,
they decided to rest by its comforting
and deep blue-green water to strategize.
How would they defeat the Wartons
and bring peace to the world?

On a walk, brilliant sunshine glimmered in the hills and stopped their conversation. They decided to check it out.

Climbing over boulders and through brush,
branches scratched the journey across their skin.

As Martine reached for the next crevice in the rock cliff, she felt a smooth surface but couldn't see it.

Standing on Carter's shoulders, Martine was surprised to see a sparkling heart-shaped object. Gently turning it back and forth, Martine wiggled the heart free.

After Carter safely helped her down,
they found a rock to sit on and began to
inspect the heart. As they rubbed its
smooth surface, their hands grew warm.

The heart started to vibrate and they heard a hum from the forest.

The heart grew warmer and began to glow with a vibrant bright green energy that slowly surrounded them.

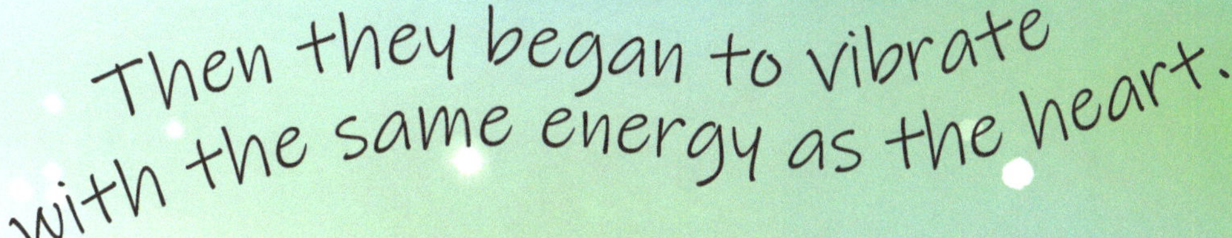

Then they began to vibrate
with the same energy as the heart.

Smiling, they stared at each other.
With the heart in their hands,
Martine and Carter felt joy, love,
and connected to everything.

Without speaking, they knew they
needed to return the heart.

The heart was energized
by its place in nature
because nature is Divine.

The Divine is in all things
and connects all things.

This green heart
had re-activated their
center of Divine love.

Martine and Carter knew
they were changed forever
and could spread this
new energy and awareness
with others,
without taking the heart.

By the time they climbed down to the Artemis Spring,
it was dark. They built a fire near the water and ate
freshly caught fish and ripe red berries.

As the sun rose, rustling in the leaves activated their war training and fight instincts. Concerned about Wartons, they jumped to alert.

Looking around, they saw a turtle, deer, bear, porcupine, raven, and squirrel peering at them, almost smiling. They felt safe and connected like they did with the green heart.

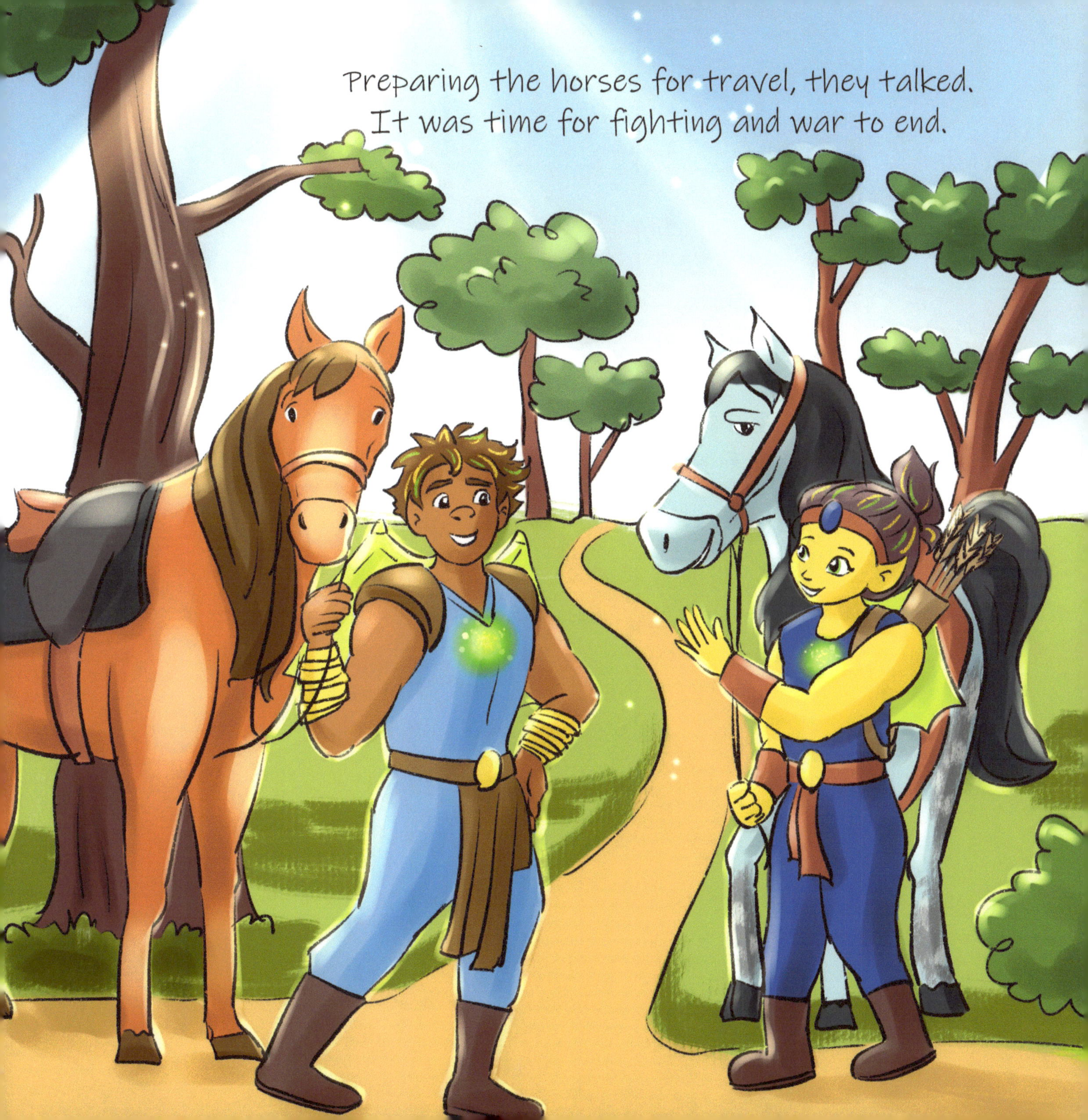
Preparing the horses for travel, they talked.
It was time for fighting and war to end.

The green heart had transformed Martine and Carter.
Their mission was different now.

They knew the power of the warm green heart energy,
of Divine love, and knew they needed to share it.

Talking about their experiences, Martine and Carter
realized that what we give to others (and even
ourselves) is what we get in return.

Going forward, they would greet everyone they
encountered—especially Wartons—with compassion,
kindness, curiosity, and love instead of hate and arrows.

Carter said, "You know...until peace prevails,
we may still have to protect and defend
ourselves and others. How do we do that
while being true to kindness and love?"

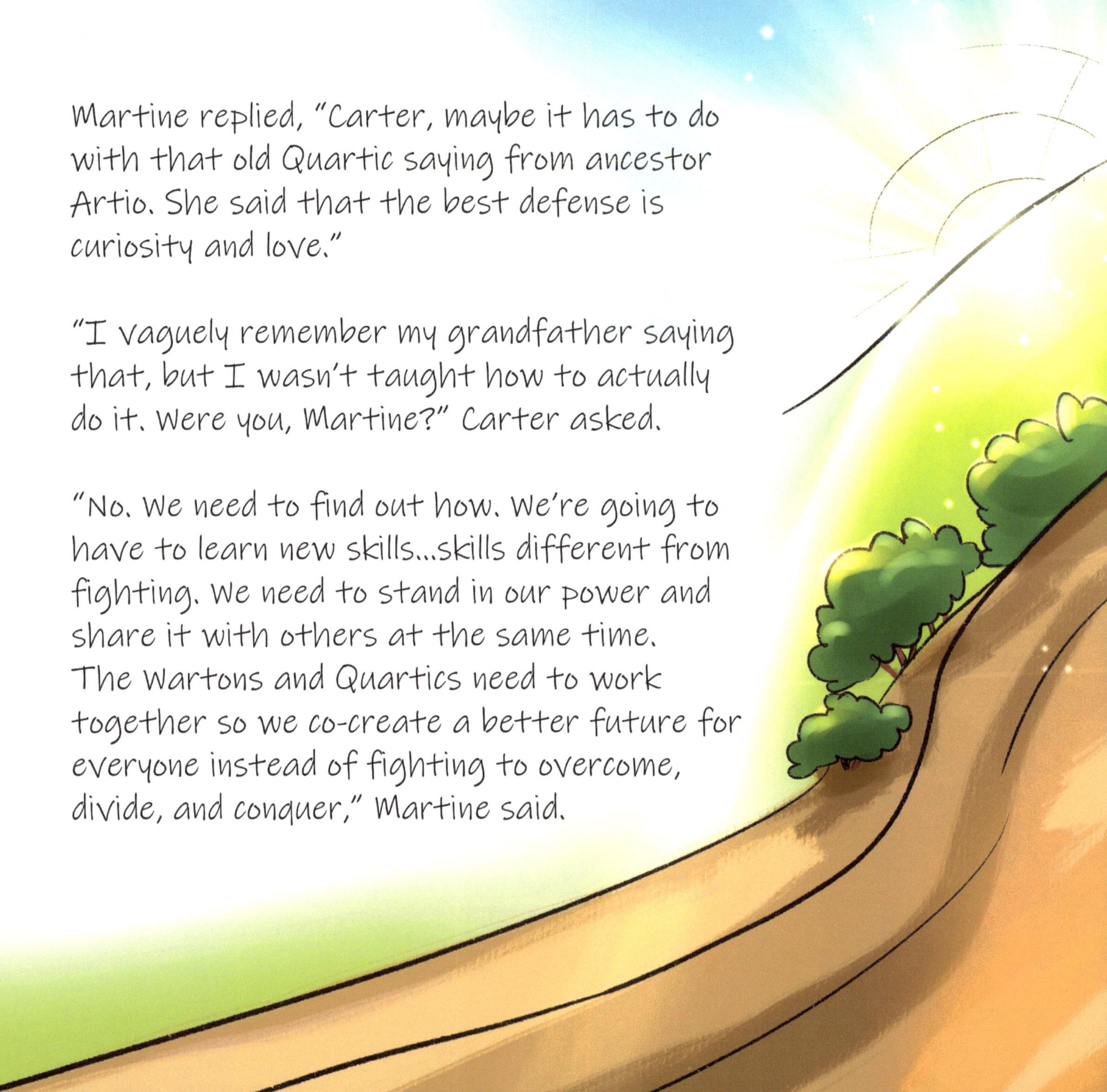

Martine replied, "Carter, maybe it has to do with that old Quartic saying from ancestor Artio. She said that the best defense is curiosity and love."

"I vaguely remember my grandfather saying that, but I wasn't taught how to actually do it. Were you, Martine?" Carter asked.

"No. We need to find out how. We're going to have to learn new skills...skills different from fighting. We need to stand in our power and share it with others at the same time. The Wartons and Quartics need to work together so we co-create a better future for everyone instead of fighting to overcome, divide, and conquer," Martine said.

"This is going to be much harder than the path we've been on, Martine. The fire of hate and anger burns and spreads easily," Carter sighed.

"I know, Carter," Martine said. "And, now we know that, once felt, once experienced, love has the power to transform hate and anger. We must do this. This is the way we human better together."

So they did.

As they spread love, it multiplied

and became our path to peace.

Anahata, the Heart Chakra

Most of us normally think of red when we think of the heart. What's up with the green heart, you ask?

In Eastern philosophical traditions, we have seven chakras or energy centers. The chakras align with the acronym ROYGBIV, which we use to help remember colors of the rainbow. The heart chakra, Anahata, is associated with the color green.

The heart chakra is our center of compassion, care, and healing. It is our source of light and love—human love, agape love, and Divine love.

For Christians, Jesus said that God is love and the kingdom of God is within. Whether you use God, the Divine, Source, Universe, or another term, this source and center of love resides within us, in our heart chakras.

When we connect with this Divine love within us and between us, we multiply the effects of love. Giving love, kindness, and compassion to ourselves and others is our way of honoring the Divine in each of us.

When we harm ourselves and others, we are harmful to the Divine in each of us.

Everyone has a choice for how they treat themselves and others.

Will you choose hate and arrows or will you choose curiosity, kindness, compassion, and love?

Make an Impact

Visit **www.ALCEMIS.com/thegreenheart** for information about how we're making an impact and how you can too. Start now with the discussion questions below. Reflect and use a journal to capture your insights. Engage in respectful discussion with friends, family, classmates, or in a community setting. Be love. Spread love.

Discussion Questions

- Who are the Wartons in your life?
    - What do these Wartons do that cause you harm or pain?

- How do you respond to the Wartons in your life?
    - What happens when you express anger or hate to a Warton?
    - What happens when you are curious about a Warton and ask questions?
    - What happens when you express caring, compassion, and loving-kindness to a Warton?

- It's hard to imagine, yet many of us do this. How might you be a Warton to yourself?
    - How might you feel if you showed yourself compassion, kindness, and love instead of judging or being mean and angry at yourself?

- How might sharing what's important to you and what you need — in a respectful way — improve your relationship with a Warton?

- If you're being attacked by a Warton, how might you turn a defensive action into curiosity and/or kindness to move the exchange forward positively?

Visit **www.ALCEMIS.com/thegreenheart** for more discussion questions as well as tools to improve communication and relationships with the Wartons in your life.

Author Note

I wrote the original version of *The Green Heart: Our Path to Peace* in 2012. A purely creative experiment, it started with a curiosity about how many words I could write in a short time that included the word art. I'd seen several yard signs over the previous days saying "Earth without art is just eh." Looking at my list, I wondered what story I could write with those words. *The Green Heart* flowed from my pen.

While I've wanted to publish this story for a long time, now may be its most relevant moment of birth. I wonder if people would have cared before, as much as I wonder about how many will care now. All the same, I'm reminded of a Cherokee legend of two wolves.

In the legend (as I recall), a grandfather is talking with his grandson about the wolves battling inside himself and within everyone — the good wolf and the bad wolf. The bad wolf focuses on fear, anger, envy, hatred, regret, arrogance, sadness, lies, greed, power over and power under, war, violence, and ego. The good wolf focuses on joy, love, humility, compassion, kindness, courage, peace, empathy, power with, truth, and generosity. The grandson asks, "Which wolf wins?" The grandfather replies, "The one you feed."

Good or bad. Peace or war. Love or hate. The "wolf" that wins is the one you feed…it's a choice. Yes, I know. Choice can feel like a battle inside, a "tug-of-war," and a churning of emotions. I've been there. I am there. I will be there again. So will you. So will all of us.

I'm also reminded of the wisdom of Viktor E. Frankl who tells us that our last human freedom is choice. We get to choose our attitude, our outlook, our beliefs, and our ways of being and doing. We can choose the ways of the bad wolf or the ways of the good wolf. It's up to each one of us.

Please choose well. We all depend upon each other for the choices we make.

About the Author

Growing up in rural Minnesota, I yearned to get far away. I never felt like I belonged. I felt unloved, unwanted, and unsafe to be me. I've been on a long journey of unpacking why, what, and how and…healing.

In my mid-20s, I was involved in a Ramsey County initiative to prevent workplace violence. I learned that oppression, simply put, is people harming people. Over the years, I'd randomly find my notes with that definition. The words would tug at me, but I didn't understand the relevance for my life until many years later.

Several years ago, when I worked to reimagine my life vision and mission, I realized I'd been pushing away my own experiences of being oppressed. Oppression is often subtle and ultimately destructive to the self and others. Oppression, discrimination, and violence exist in relationships, families, communities, religious and non-profit organizations, and the workplace. When I wrote my vision, I acknowledged that breaking open and transforming oppressive thinking and systems for freedom, peace, healing, and positive impact is intricately related to my purpose and my work as a change consultant and leadership coach.

I've had a lot of healing and personal growth since writing my vision, and in incredibly profound ways. Healing takes courage. It's painful to dig deep, acknowledge what has happened and why, and make tough choices for new ways of being and doing.

My life is richer today because of choices I've made for partnership instead of domination. Beyond the partnership I'm developing with myself, the most rewarding partnership I have is with my husband. Since meeting in 2020, we continue to find ways of relating well and living out the power of the green heart, even if we do so imperfectly. We love co-creating our life together, including navigating the messy moments with dance, laughter, and love.

About the Illustrator

Melitopol, my hometown, is currently under occupation but holds many memories for me. Since childhood, I loved drawing, inspired by my favorite actor, Johnny Depp, and the enchanting Disney style. Despite my passion for art, my parents encouraged a stable career, leading me to graduate in architecture. After several years in the field, I realized life had other paths for me.

Moving to Kyiv, I embraced motherhood and entered a period of self-discovery. I explored bilingual education, learned the Shichida method, crafted with polymer clay, and studied nutrition. One day, reflecting on my purpose through Ikigai, I discovered digital illustration, which opened the door to children's book illustration.

My journey has been a winding path filled with thorns, yet it has also been a source of strength during the darkest times — not only in my life but also for my country as we faced the invasion that changed everything. Each Ukrainian felt the weight of this conflict; I know firsthand that when the full-scale war began, we traversed through all stages of grief.

Now, after four long years, I can say that we have adapted to living in a state of war where every moment could be our last. Perhaps it is precisely because of this that we cherish life even more and refuse to put off what truly matters.

Yet, amidst all these lessons learned, one thing remains clear: we long for peace and a calm sky above our heads. As I continue to create illustrations that inspire joy and wonder in children, I hold onto the hope that, one day, our world will be filled with laughter and tranquility once more.

Gratitude

Thank you for your partnership, my dear husband. Your support, encouragement, and love bring me great joy. To my beta readers—Megan Rounds, Liz Nicklos, Joan Steffend Brandmeier, and Shelly Swanson—I am grateful for your insightful and gracious feedback. For your excitement and supportive words, thank you Marilyn Carlson Nelson. Connie Anderson and the Women of Words (WOW) community have provided an encouraging and informative network of support over many years, and I'm honored to be a member. Cynthia Wold, thank you for the many opportunities to write and share in the safe space of pure expression. John Currie, thank you for the inspiring color idea. Thank you Manja Pach from the Etty Hillesum Centrum for providing Etty's original quote in Dutch. To Pastor Martinson, from your place in the infinite presence of Divine love, may your soul know how your gentle kindness to me as a small child in pain rippled positively through my life; "God" is love and the "kingdom" is within. The manifestation of *The Green Heart* story in its colorful glory has been a rewarding collaboration with the incredibly talented, positive, and resilient Juliet Frost. Her creativity and courage inspires me. May the loving spirit of the green heart in action bring us all peace.

~ Laura

I would like to extend my deepest gratitude to the author, Laura, for inviting me to illustrate a book that seeks to unite and spread peace rather than war. It is my fervent hope that this book becomes prophetic for Ukraine and Russia, serving as a beacon of hope and understanding. I am also profoundly thankful to my family—my husband and children—for their unwavering support and motivation as I navigate my path of purpose. Your love fuels my creativity and inspires me every day. Lastly, I want to express my appreciation to everyone who carries the message of peace and love into this world. It is a necessity that we all embrace, especially in these challenging times. Together, let us sow the seeds of harmony and understanding, for our world needs it now more than ever.

~ Juliet

"Dit is eigenlijk onze enige morele
taak: in zichzelf grote vlaktes van rust
ontginnen, steeds meer rust, zodat
men deze rust weer uitstralen kan
naar de anderen. En hoe meer rust er in
de mensen is, des te rustiger zal het
ook in deze opgewonden wereld zijn."
~ Etty Hillesum
(dinsdag 29 sept. 1942)

"This is, basically, our only moral task:
to cultivate vast expanses of peace
within ourselves, ever more peace, so
that we can radiate this peace to
others. And the more peace there is
within people, the more peaceful it will
be in this tumultuous world."
~ Etty Hillesum
(tuesday, sept. 29, 1942)